Sister of
the Bride

LISA BRUCE

Illustrated by
DUNCAN SMITH

HEINEMANN·LONDON

First published in 1995 by Heinemann Young Books
an imprint of Egmont Children's Books Limited
Michelin House, 81 Fulham Rd, London SW3 6RB

ISBN 0 434 97211 8

Reprinted 1998

Text © Lisa Bruce 1995
Illustrations © Duncan Smith 1995

Printed in Italy by Olivotto

A school pack of BANANAS 79-84
is available from
Heinemann Educational Books
ISBN 0 435 00097 7

CHAPTER 1

JASSY WAS WOKEN early by the sun
streaming through a gap in her
bedroom curtains. At first she didn't
know where she was. Why was her
Aunty Jagdeep snoring peacefully in
her bed, while she lay on the floor next
to her cousin, Jamila? For a while Jassy
stared at a sunbeam dancing on the
white ceiling. Then she remembered -
today was to be her sister, Manjit's,
wedding day. Jassy was suddenly wide

awake and filled with excitement. She didn't want to waste a minute of this very special day, so she quickly got up, washed and dressed and made her way to the kitchen for some breakfast.

All over the house relatives from up and down the country were curled up in chairs, on sofas or sleeping mats. By the time Jassy had finished her puris, the kitchen was bustling with people: guests talking and laughing, children shouting and babies crying.

For hours Jassy's mother was kept busy making sure that everyone had breakfast. Only when people began to go and put on their wedding clothes was she able to sit down for a quiet

cup of tea.

In the small bedroom at the top of the house, a whole team of aunts and cousins began dressing Manjit, doing her hair, and putting on her make-up. Jassy was just about to go and watch, when she heard her Aunty Surjit

calling her:

'Jassy! Jassy! Take Rajinder to his Dhadi, will you?'

Aunty Surjit handed over her lively three-year-old before disappearing into the small bedroom with a tray of eye shadow. Jassy looked down at the little boy, who promptly stuck his tongue out at her. Jassy sighed.

'Come on then,' she said.

'No.'

She tried again, tugging his hand.

'Let's go and find Dhadi, Rajinder.'

'Won't,' he screamed. He broke away and ran downstairs towards the open front door.

Outside on the street Rajinder's father was carefully winding the bright, joyful red ribbon around the front of the gleaming white wedding car. He glanced up when he saw his little son heading towards him.

'Jassy, take Rajinder inside, will you?
I'm busy out here!'

Jassy muttered under her breath as
she caught up with the troublesome
little boy. Why did she always get
lumbered with the job of looking after
the younger children?

Rajinder was strong for his age and
struggled when Jassy tried to pick him
up. She had to half drag him back into
the house. She found Rajinder's elderly
Grandmother sitting in the corner of
the kitchen.

'Here's your Dhadi,' she said sweetly as she put him down on the old lady's lap. 'Now, you be a good boy and play nicely on her knee.'

Jassy guessed that he wouldn't, but at least he would not be her problem any more.

Jassy decided to try again to see what Manjit was looking like, so she wandered up to the small bedroom.

That was a mistake, for there were too many people there already and Rajinder, who was looking for his mother, followed Jassy in through the door.

Having children in there was more than the army of make-up artists could bear.

'Out! Out of here!' they yelled with one voice.

'Jassy! Take Rajinder and go and wait in the car,' ordered Aunty Surjit.

'Please, Jassy,' pleaded a panicky Manjit through her half-painted face.

Jassy didn't want to spoil her sister's wedding day, so for once she bit her tongue and did as she was told. Picking up the struggling toddler, she marched towards the white wedding car and dumped Rajinder on the back seat. Then Jassy climbed in herself and sat down, carefully arranging the folds of her new yellow suit so that they would not crease.

Rajinder was delighted to be in the car. He climbed straight into the front seat and began to play at driving, by swinging on the steering wheel and making loud *brrrm brrrm* noises. Jassy paid no attention to him whatsoever.

She folded her hands together underneath her flimsy golden chunni and gazed out of the window trying to look as dignified and grown-up as possible.

Jassy didn't notice when Rajinder grew bored playing with the wheel. She didn't see when he found the bunch of keys his father had left dangling in the ignition. She paid no attention when the little boy waved the keys happily out of the half-open window. And she certainly had no idea that Rajinder had dropped the keys, because as they fell from his hands he accidentally made contact with the horn.

Blarrr went the horn.

'Stop it, Rajinder!' shouted Jassy.

In all that noise she had no chance of hearing the tinkle of the keys as they hit the grate underneath the car, or the faint *plish* as they fell into the murky drain far below the street.

CHAPTER 2

JASSY THOUGHT ALL was well. She began to smile as the front door of her house was flung open and Manjit came out in her red and gold saree. The jewels in her nose, hair and ears glittered magically in the early morning sunlight. Jassy had never before seen anyone looking so beautiful.

Slowly the procession of video cameraman, bride, and relatives wound their way down the garden path. The neighbours hung over their gates to see the wedding party leave. Manjit was helped into the car.

'Good luck, Manjit,' whispered Jassy.

Manjit grinned.

The rest of the relatives piled into the remaining cars and drove off. It was then that the trouble *really* began. Uncle Jaspal settled himself into the driver's seat and turned to smile at Jassy, Manjit, their mother and father. Rajinder was travelling with his own mother in a different car, much to Jassy's relief.

'Right, let's be off then,' said Uncle Jaspal cheerily, his turban bobbing from side to side. He leaned forwards to start the car.

'What the...!' he began. 'Where are the keys?'

Uncle Jaspal patted all over his clothes to make sure that they weren't still in one of his pockets. Then he turned to Jassy.

'I left the keys in the car, I'm sure I did. Where are they, Jassy?'

Jassy shrugged. She didn't know anything about the car keys, which was true. However, this was not enough to satisfy the grown-ups. Soon every person in the car began questioning Jassy about the keys.

'You must have let Rajinder take them!' her father yelled.

'For goodness' sake, couldn't you have paid more attention to what he was doing!' shrieked her mother. 'You were meant to be looking after him.'

'You do realise that we can't go anywhere now,' Uncle Jaspal growled.

Manjit, wrapped in her splendid red and gold chunni simply sat in the corner of the luxurious car and cried.

'Stop that, Manjit,' ordered her mother. 'Now look what you have done, Jassy. She'll ruin all her make-up.'

She looked fiercely at her youngest daughter.

Everybody in the wedding car got out. By this time all the other guests had departed and Jassy's family stood on the pavement gazing at the gleaming but now useless wedding car. Manjit began to sob louder.

CHAPTER 3

'YOU LOOK LIKE people with a problem,' came a friendly voice from across the street.

It was Johnny who lived at No. 10. He was setting off for work.

'Can I help at all?' he asked.

Johnny was a mini cab driver and he drove a clapped-out, lime green car with a large sign on the roof which read MAXI TAXI in bold letters.

'Need a lift do you?'

'Yes please,' Jassy's flustered father

gulped reluctantly. 'We are urgently needing to be at a wedding.'

'Hop in quick then. I'll get you there in a jiffy,' grinned Johnny, opening the taxi door.

It was a dreadful squeeze in the back of Johnny's cab. There was no way that Jassy could avoid her new suit being crumpled. Her mother, too, looked angry as she tried to stop her wedding finery from being crushed. At least Manjit was all right, she sat in the front seat with her beautiful red saree spread around her.

All the way to the Gurdwara no one spoke to Jassy. Johnny was thanked by everyone for his help, and he in turn made polite conversation, but none of them spoke to Jassy.

They think it's my fault, thought Jassy, *and it was nothing to do with me.*

CHAPTER 4

THE TAXI SWUNG into the large
Gurdwara car park and pulled up in
front of the steps of the white domed
building. Already crowds of anxious
guests stood by the entrance, looking at
their watches and wondering where the
bride was.

Jassy could hear the gasp of
astonishment as the shabby taxi door
opened and they saw the bride.

Manjit hissed to Jassy as she climbed out:

'I'll never forgive you for this, *never*.'

Straightening her skirts she lowered her eyes and became at once the dutiful, calm and serene bride.

Everyone was annoyed with Jassy. As each of the grown-ups from the car explained to the other guests, the tale became more and more twisted. Jassy even overheard one guest whispering that Jassy had *deliberately* hidden the keys because she was jealous of Manjit.

Jassy was furious and wanted to shout at everybody, to tell them that it was not her fault. But she knew that it would not do any good. No one would believe her and she would only get into even more trouble for being a nuisance.

Jassy sat cross-legged on the floor of

the worship room in the Gurdwara beside her mother and Aunty Jagdeep. No one spoke to her, which was just as well for Jassy was trying to hold back her tears. She must not cry at Manjit's wedding, she mustn't.

The four musicians in the corner struck up the opening chords of a hymn and Jassy's mother threw her a stern *don't you dare do anything to let me down* look.

At the end of the hymn Manjit appeared. Guided by her cousin Kuldip, she walked demurely down the centre of the room, her eyes lowered respectfully.

Everyone looked on admiringly as Manjit glided gracefully to her position beside Kulvant. She looked radiant, like a princess. Jassy gazed at her sister wondrously. You would never have

guessed how upset she had been only
minutes ago.

The Granthi (priest) took his place
behind the Guru Granth Sahib, the
holy book, and the ceremony began.

Usually at weddings, Jassy got bored during the two-hour-long ceremony. She often ended up playing with the other children at the back of the room. Today though was different. Today the holy readings and prayers were made special because it was her sister, Manjit, they were talking about.

Jassy was so proud as Manjit and Kulvant were tied together with the long flimsy scarf and they began their steady walk, in a circle, around the Guru Granth Sahib.

The ceremony was almost over when

disaster struck. Now Jassy often got hiccups. The hiccups usually only lasted

a few moments and usually they were quite quiet. But this time they were fast and violent.

'Hic!'

All eyes turned to stare at Jassy.

'Hic! Hic!'

Aunty Jagdeep muttered something darkly under her breath which Jassy didn't catch. And she could see Manjit wasn't pleased.

'Go and get a drink of water,' her mother whispered to her, giving her a little nudge.

Embarrassed at causing such a commotion Jassy crept out of the room and down the stairs. At the bottom she had a five-minute search before she located her new golden sandals.

'Can I help you?' the shoe attendant asked.

'Hic!' Jassy shook her head violently and fled.

CHAPTER 5

JASSY KNEW WHERE the Gurdwara
kitchens were. There the large pans of
curries and daal would be simmering
ready for the wedding meal. She
hurried through the communal Langar,
where long tables had been set out in
readiness for the guests, and gently
pushed the kitchen door open.
A sharp, acrid smell hit her, a smell like
burning! In the corner she saw a coil of

black smoke winding its way up to the ceiling. Jassy realised that something in the kitchen had caught fire. She was about to slam the door shut again when something caught her eye. It was the Granthi's sister. She must have been left to watch the food and fallen asleep in the chair.

Panic-stricken, Jassy fled to fetch help. At the bottom of the stairs she met Aunty Surjit taking Rajinder to the toilet.

'Hic! Oh, thank goodness you are here, Aunty,' Jassy panted. 'You have got to... Hic... help me.'

Aunty Surjit turned fiercely on Jassy, pointing an accusing finger at her.

'You have done enough mischief for one day, Jaswinder,' she scolded. 'Can't you see you are spoiling your sister's wedding day.'

Aunty Surjit flounced away and disappeared into the toilets.

'But...' Jassy started to speak. It was too late. Aunty Surjit had gone.

Jassy had no choice but to race upstairs into the worship room. Unfortunately she had forgotten to remove her sandals, so before she even had a chance to open her mouth an elderly attendant gripped her by the arm and frog-marched her out. Jassy started to explain, but the woman was not listening.

'You cannot wear your shoes in here. You should know better than that!' she said sternly. 'Go back downstairs and take them off.'

She too disappeared back to the ceremony leaving Jassy hiccupping helplessly on the stairs. This was an emergency. Why would no one listen to her? The Granthi's sister could die in there... Suddenly Jassy knew she had to get the old lady out somehow.

Jassy ran back to the kitchen. Without hesitation she tied her long scarf around her mouth to prevent the smoke from getting into her lungs.

After taking a deep breath of clean air Jassy ran into the room.

By now the smoke was thicker than before but Jassy could quite easily see the slumped figure of the Granthi's sister in her chair. Jassy held on to the back of the chair and pulled with all her might. It was fortunate that the Granthi's sister had a small thin body so she was not too heavy. The kitchen floor had recently been relaid with shiny tiles and the chair slid easily across the floor. It took Jassy just four massive tugs to haul the chair out into

the main room. All the time she held
her breath, which cured her hiccups,
although she had no time to notice.

Just as Jassy finally dragged the chair
out, the shoe attendant appeared.

'Aieeeee!' she shrieked when she saw
the Granthi's sister and understood the
situation. Quickly she ran over to see if
the old lady was all right. The frail
body did not move and the shoe
attendant immediately began a low
mournful wail.

'What about the fire?' spluttered
Jassy. 'All the people are upstairs. We
must do something.'

The shoe attendant was so absorbed
in her wailing that she didn't seem to
hear. Jassy realised that she would
have to fetch help herself. Her eyes
were smarting from the smoke, and her
pretty yellow suit was singed and

sooted as she stumbled out to the phone box in the car park. Lifting the heavy receiver she remembered what she had been taught and dialled 999.

'Fire, police or ambulance,' came a crisp voice, almost instantly.

'Fire,' panted Jassy urgently. 'But someone is hurt, so we may need an ambulance as well.'

The phone clicked and Jassy soon found herself talking to an officer at the fire station. She gave all the details of what she had seen and where the Gurdwara was. Jassy put down the phone. Thank goodness the fire brigade were on their way. What should she do now though? The wedding party was still inside the building. They were all in grave danger.

CHAPTER 6

JASSY RAN AS fast as she could. She ran through the car park, past the entrance to the dining room, where the shoe attendant was still wailing. She ran up the stairs, two at a time, and burst into the ceremony just as the Granthi was saying the final prayers.

'FIRE!' shouted Jassy at the top of her voice.

All the heads in the room turned towards her. For a moment Jassy paused, her face burning with embarrassment at the sudden attention of all these people. Jassy could see the anger on her mother's face which quickly turned to shock as she noticed Jassy's smoke-smudged state.

Before Jassy could say anything else, the high-pitched whoop of the fire engine siren filled the room. Everyone realised that Jassy was telling the truth. They all jumped up and made their way out of the building as quickly as possible, the older ones helped by some of the sturdy young men.

In the car park everyone huddled together, their bare feet sore on the uneven tarmac. The fire crew ran hoses into the kitchen and the fire was soon put out. An ambulance arrived to take the Granthi's sister to hospital. She was in a state of shock, and she was coughing from the smoke that she had inhaled, but the ambulance woman said that she would be all right.

CHAPTER 7

At LONG LAST the building was declared safe again and the guests trooped back inside.

'You were very lucky there,' the fire chief said to Jassy's father. 'If it hadn't been for this brave young girl here, things could have been a lot worse. We managed to catch the blaze before it had a chance to take a real hold on the building. The kitchen is black, of course, but a brisk clean-up and a spot of paint and it will be as good as new.'

Everyone looked appreciatively at Jassy.

'Please won't you stay and have a drink with us?' Jassy's father offered the fireman a glass of cola.

'Don't mind if I do,' smiled the fire chief. 'It's thirsty work fighting fires.'

A crate of soft drinks, about the only thing that had not been damaged by the smoke, was passed around and soon each guest had a glassful. Everyone chatted to the fire crew, relieved to have escaped so easily.

Jassy was the centre of attention. Time and time again she was asked to tell how she had rescued the Granthi's sister. When the fire chief asked why she had gone to the kitchen, Jassy explained about the troubles of the day starting with the car keys, the ride in the taxi and finally her hiccups.

'I see,' said the fire chief thoughtfully. 'It was lucky the fire was only just taking hold. You should never, never go into a room filled with smoke if you can't see across the room. It's extremely dangerous, the fumes could kill you. But you did well to act so quickly. You were very brave.'

Then he moved away to whisper mysteriously in some of the other fire officers' ears. They each nodded.

Some of the firemen walked up to Manjit and Kulvant.

'Ah-hem,' coughed the middle one,
importantly. 'As you haven't exactly got
any transport, can we give you a lift
anywhere in our vehicle?'

The newly-weds looked at each other
and smiled.

Jassy's father stood up on a chair and
announced that the bridal couple would
soon be leaving. As the food had all
been burnt he promised to throw a
huge party in the Gurdwara when the

happy couple came back from their
honeymoon. Everyone was invited,
including the fire crew.

A huge crowd gathered outside in
the car park to watch Manjit and
Kulvant depart. They clambered on
board the enormous fire engine and
waved happily at everybody. At the last
moment, Manjit grasped Jassy's hand
and pulled her up beside her.

'We can't leave without the heroine,
can we?'

Jassy was thrilled. She had never been in a fire engine before.

'Oh, Manjit,' she sighed throwing her arms around her sister. 'I am so sorry about spoiling your day.'

'Nonsense!' Manjit and Kulvant said together. '*You* are the one who *saved* the day.'

With that, the fire engine tooted good-bye to everyone and slowly pulled out of the car park in front of the cheering crowd.

WORDS THAT YOU MAY NOT KNOW

Chunni	scarf
Daal	lentil dish
Granthi	priest
Gurdwara	Sikh Temple
Guru Granth Sahib	Sikh holy book written by many gurus
Langar	communal dining room
Puris	flat dried bread